This book belongs to:

_____

_____

_____

Rooster Wore Skinny Jeans
is an original concept by
© Jessie Miller

Illustrator: Barbara Bakos
Represented by Bright Illustration

First Published in the UK in 2017 by
MAVERICK ARTS PUBLISHING LTD

Maverick
arts publishing

Studio 3A, City Business Centre, 6 Brighton Road,
Horsham, West Sussex, RH13 5BB
© Maverick Arts Publishing Limited 2017
+44 (0)1403 256941

distributed by **Lerner**

American edition published in 2018 by Maverick Arts Publishing,
distributed in the United States and Canada by Lerner Publishing
Group Inc., 241 First Avenue North, Minneapolis, MN 55401 USA

ISBN 978-1-84886-313-2

Rooster
Wore
Skinny
Jeans

Written by
Jessie Miller

Illustrated by
Barbara Bakos

On a typical Wednesday at **Rosemary Mill**,
A countryside farm run by old Farmer Phil,

The rooster was making his rounds in the coop,

When a brown paper package arrived on the stoop.

He thought, "There's no way! It's too soon! It can't be!
I just ordered them Monday... the shipping was free!"
He eagerly tip-toed his way to the door,
Then bent down to pick up his box from the floor.

He tore off the tape with a **big** cheesy grin,
Then marvelled in awe at the contents within.
The sparkling **stitching**, a **striking gold** hue!

The indigo **denim**, a **dazzling** blue!

"The **Flattering** rise and the **slimming** design,
Not too loose, not too snug... these jeans are **divine!**"

He went through the farm with a confident stride.

He felt like a **king**. He had nothing to hide!

"The others will love the new jeans that I've bought!"

Their reaction, however, was not what he'd thought.

At first there were **stares**, a few **snickers**, a leer.
Then the crow taunted loudly for others to hear.

They **howled** in laughter and whistled his name,
As the rooster ran off, his face burning with shame.

He hid in the barn on a tall bale of hay,
Hoping the others would just go away.

He caught a quick glance of himself from behind,
And suddenly **everything** cleared in his mind.

"What's not to love? Are they being **sarcastic**?
These jeans are amazing; my butt looks fantastic!"

He calmed himself down, let the bad feelings sink,

Then he thought, "You know what? I don't care what they think!

I wanted these jeans, and I bought them for **me**.

Their opinions don't matter. I'll show them! They'll see!"

He flew to the top of the barn in a streak,
Stood as tall as he could on the uppermost peak.

Cock a doodle doo!

He brushed off all feelings of **worry** and **doubt**,
Then he **cockled** and **doodled** and **dooed** with a shout!

A chicken spoke out with her head towards the sky,
"I kind of **admire** the nerve of that guy...
He won't be held back by the things that we say,
He is being **himself**, and I think that's okay."

The animals **cheered** and encouraged his call,
And the rooster, he **beamed** at the sight of it all.

Later that night, as the farm lay to rest,
The rooster pre-ordered a **gold sequined vest**.